MAGIC TREE HOUSE®

#33 NARWHAL ON A SUNNY NIGHT

Dear Reader,

Did you know there's a Magic Tree House® book for every kid? From those just starting to read chapter books to more experienced readers, Magic Tree House® has something for everyone, including science, sports, geography, wildlife, history... and always a bit of mystery and magic!

Magic Tree House®
Adventures with Jack and Annie, perfect for readers who are just starting to read chapter books.
F&P Level: M

**Magic Tree House®
Merlin Missions**
More challenging adventures for the experienced Magic Tree House® reader.
F&P Levels: M–N

**Magic Tree House®
Super Edition**
A longer and more dangerous adventure with Jack and Annie.
F&P Level: P

**Magic Tree House®
Fact Trackers**
Nonfiction companions to your favorite Magic Tree House® adventures.
F&P Levels: N–X

Happy reading!

Mary Pope Osborne

MAGIC TREE HOUSE®

#33 NARWHAL ON A SUNNY NIGHT

BY MARY POPE OSBORNE

ILLUSTRATED BY AG FORD

A STEPPING STONE BOOK™

Random House New York

Text copyright © 2020 by Mary Pope Osborne
Jacket art and interior illustrations copyright © 2020 by AG Ford

All rights reserved. Published in the United States by Random House Children's Books, a division of Penguin Random House LLC, New York.

Random House and the colophon are registered trademarks and A Stepping Stone Book and the colophon are trademarks of Penguin Random House LLC.

Magic Tree House is a registered trademark of Mary Pope Osborne; used under license.

Visit us on the Web!
rhcbooks.com
MagicTreeHouse.com

Educators and librarians, for a variety of teaching tools,
visit us at RHTeachersLibrarians.com

Library of Congress Cataloging-in-Publication Data
Names: Osborne, Mary Pope, author. | Ford, AG, illustrator.
Title: Narwhal on a sunny night / by Mary Pope Osborne; illustrated by AG Ford.
Description: New York: Random House, [2020] | Series: Magic tree house; #33 | "A Stepping Stone Book." | Summary: "The magic tree house whisks Jack and Annie away to Greenland, where they discover they've traveled back in time to meet Leif Erikson" —Provided by publisher.
Identifiers: LCCN 2019018578 | ISBN 978-0-525-64836-9 (hardcover) | ISBN 978-0-525-64837-6 (lib. bdg.) | ISBN 978-0-525-64838-3 (ebook)
Subjects: | CYAC: Time travel—Fiction. | Leiv Eiríksson, d. ca. 1020—Fiction. | Vikings—Fiction. | Narwhal—Fiction. | Magic—Fiction. | Tree houses—Fiction. | Greenland—History—To 1500—Fiction. Classification: LCC PZ7.O81167 Nar 2020 | DDC [Fic]—dc23

Printed in the United States of America
10 9 8 7 6 5 4 3 2 1

This book has been officially leveled by using the F&P Text Level Gradient™ Leveling System.

Random House Children's Books supports the First Amendment and celebrates the right to read.

To Rose Schwartz,
with deepest thanks

CONTENTS

1

GREEN-LAND

Jack and Annie sat on their porch in the warm summer twilight. Jack was reading a library book called *Amazing Facts.*

"Get this," he said. "A beehive can have as many as sixty million bees in it."

"Is that all?" Annie said.

"Ha," said Jack. "Okay, then get this!" He read: "Some experts say there might be ten billion *trillion* stars in the universe."

"Wrong," said Annie. "In fact, there are ten billion trillion and seventy-three."

Jack laughed. They both looked up at the dark-blue sky. The first stars were coming out.

"Seriously, ten billion trillion . . . ?" said Annie. "I can't even imagine it." She stood up. "Hey, do you see that?"

"What?" said Jack.

"That little cloud," Annie said.

"Where?" said Jack, standing.

"Over the treetops," said Annie.

"Oh, man," whispered Jack. He saw it, too: a small, brightly glowing cloud over the Frog Creek woods.

"We'd better check it out," said Annie.

Jack put his book on a porch chair. "Mom? Dad?" he called through the screen door. "We'll be back soon!"

"Fifteen minutes!" their dad called. "We'll watch a movie together!"

"Great!" called Jack. He grabbed his backpack and then turned to Annie. "Let's go. Hurry!"

Jack and Annie dashed down the porch steps. They tore across their yard and headed up the sidewalk.

When they came to the Frog Creek woods, they crossed the street and hurried between the trees.

The darkening woods were filled with the sounds of crickets and frogs. The air smelled of warm green leaves and wood and earth.

Soon Jack and Annie came to the tallest oak.

"Hurray!" said Annie.

The magic tree house was back. It was shimmering against the evening sky.

"Yes!" said Jack. He grabbed the rope ladder and started up. Annie followed. They climbed into the tree house.

"Look," said Jack. In the last light of day, he saw a book on the floor.

He grabbed the book. He read the title on the plain green cover.

GREENLAND
The World's Largest Island

"Greenland!" said Annie. "That sounds nice!"

"Yeah, our teacher told us about Greenland," said Jack. "But I don't remember what he said...."

"Open the book," said Annie.

Jack opened the book. He found a map in a pocket on the inside cover. He took it out and unfolded it.

Everything was black-and-white, except for Greenland. The huge island was colored green.

"*Green*-land sounds so beautiful," said Annie. "Like it's filled with green grass and green trees."

"Don't be fooled. It can't be very green," said Jack.

"Why not?" said Annie.

"Because, look." With his finger, Jack traced a circle on the map. "This is the Arctic Circle. Inside

5

the circle is most of Greenland, Norway, Iceland, and parts of Canada and Russia. It's one of the coldest regions in the world."

"Oh. Then why is the island called Greenland?" asked Annie.

Jack shrugged. "And why are we going there?" he said. "Do you see anything from Morgan?"

They looked around the tree house again.

"Here!" said Annie. She picked up a small piece of yellow paper. She read aloud:

On your next journey
You will land on the shore
Of an island with icebergs,
Reindeer, and more.

On a day that seems endless,
With no dark of night,
Travel through fog.
Travel through light.

Explore different worlds.
Show friends where to go.
Unite all these worlds
With a word that will glow.

"*No dark of night?*" said Jack. "What does that mean?"

"I don't know," said Annie. "And what about: *Unite all these worlds with a word that will glow?*"

"Yeah, what word?" said Jack. "It sounds really cold, too, with 'icebergs, reindeer, and more.'"

"But that could be fun," said Annie. "We can handle cold. Remember our great trip to the Arctic a while ago?"

"Oh, right," said Jack. "We wore those polar bear masks."

"And saved the baby bears," said Annie. "*That* was fun, right?"

"Yeah, it was," said Jack. "Okay! Back to the cold!"

7

Annie pointed at the green island on their map. "I wish we could go there!" she said.

The wind started to blow.

The tree house started to spin.

It spun faster and faster.

Then everything was still.

Absolutely still.

2

ICE EVERYWHERE

Sunlight shone through the tree house window. The sound of splashing water came from outside.

"Hey, it doesn't feel that cold," said Annie.

"Maybe because we're wearing these heavy woolen clothes," said Jack.

Their summer clothes had changed into wool outfits. Now they had on thick wool coats, wool shirts, wool caps, wool mittens, and wool pants. Even Jack's backpack had changed into a wool bag. His notebook and pencil were inside.

"You were right," said Annie, looking out the window. "I don't see much green here."

Jack looked out with her. The tree house had landed on the rocky shore of an ocean bay. Across the water were brown mountains with snow-white peaks.

The air felt crisp and clean. Seagulls swooped low over sparkling blue seawater. The sun shined on sheets of ice.

"Ready to explore?" said Annie.

"Yep," said Jack.

Jack slipped their map back inside the Greenland book. He put the book and Morgan's rhyme in the wool bag.

Then he and Annie climbed out the window. They stepped onto a pebbly shore.

"Oh, man, ice *everywhere*," said Jack.

The ocean bay was filled with ice. Small flat icebergs were floating in the middle of the bay. Others were close to shore.

"The water must be freezing," said Annie.

Jack took off a glove and dipped his hand into the seawater. "Ow!" he yelped. "It's so cold, it hurts!"

Jack dried his hand and put his glove back on. Then he took out the Greenland book. He read aloud from the first page:

For millions of years, Greenland has been mostly covered with ice. In the twenty-first century, experts worry that the world's climate is warming and the ice is melting. Scientists from different countries live at research stations in Greenland to study the effects of climate change.

"Now I remember what my teacher told us," said Jack. "Melting ice in the Arctic can cause sea levels to rise and lead to disaster."

"That's serious," said Annie. "I hope we meet some scientists."

"Me too," said Jack. "I wonder who else lives here." He found a section in the book called "People of Greenland." He read:

Experts believe that people first occupied Greenland about 4,500 years ago. Today 56,000 people live on the island. Most of them are known as the Inuit (say IN-u-it).

"Inuit!" said Annie. "Like the Inuit seal hunter we met on our other Arctic trip! He was great."

"Yeah, but I don't see any signs of Inuit people in this area," said Jack. He looked around at the cold, barren landscape. "It feels pretty lonely."

"Wait, look at *that*!" said Annie. She pointed to a group of small silver-gray creatures resting on an iceberg.

"I think those are seals?" said Jack.

"They're so little and cute," said Annie.

Jack found a chapter on seals in the book. He read:

Greenland has three kinds of ice seals. Ringed seals are the smallest.

"Okay, they must be *ringed* seals!" said Jack.

Suddenly the seals let out high-pitched barks. They spun their heads from side to side. Then they slipped off the ice and disappeared into the water.

"I think we scared them," said Jack.

A swooshing sound came from across the bay.

"Not *us*!" cried Annie. "A *whale*!"

A huge gray whale was skimming across the

water. A sharp burst of air spurted out the blow-hole on top of its head.

"Whoa!" said Jack.

The whale leapt into the air. Then it crashed down with a giant splash. It dove under the sea.

"A humpback! That was a humpback!" said Annie. "I saw the bump on its back. Humpback whales sing. They sing a different song every year!"

"How do you know that?" said Jack.

"I love whales! I wrote a report on them," said Annie.

"Great," said Jack. He looked up *whales* in the index of their book. He found the right page and read aloud:

Greenland's waters are filled with whales. Fifteen different kinds can be seen along its coasts and in ocean inlets. They include humpback whales, orcas, narwhals, beluga whales—

"Wait! More whales!" cried Annie. "A bunch more!"

"I know," said Jack, not looking up from the book. "There are fifteen kinds." He kept reading:

fin whales, blue whales—

"Stop! I mean more in *real life*!" shouted Annie. "Look up, Jack!"

Jack looked up.

He couldn't believe his eyes. About a dozen whales were swimming in the bay now. They had sleek gray backs. Each had a long tusk jutting from its rounded head.

"Narwhals!" shouted Annie. "*Real* narwhals!"

3

UNICORNS OF THE SEA

The narwhals were bounding through the water. Foamy waves washed over the ice.

"I wrote about narwhals in my report!" said Annie. "They're some of the most mysterious creatures on earth!" She ran down the pebbly shore to get a closer look.

Clutching the book and his bag, Jack ran after her.

"They're called the Unicorns of the Sea!" Annie shouted over her shoulder.

"I get it!" called Jack. Their long horns looked just like the horns of unicorns!

The narwhals arched out of the water to breathe the fresh air. As they exhaled, puffs of mist burst from their blowholes, like sneezes.

Annie stopped running. "Their horns are really tusks. And almost all narwhals with tusks are male," she said, panting. "And the tusk is a super-long tooth. It can be as long as ten feet!"

"No kidding, a ten-foot tooth?" said Jack. "What does the tooth do?" He'd heard of narwhals before, but he didn't know much about them.

"No one knows for sure," said Annie. "Scientists hardly ever see narwhals. But we just got here, and there they are! I don't believe it!"

"We're lucky," said Jack.

He opened their book. He found a section on narwhals and read aloud:

Narwhals are mysterious whales that live most of their lives in the dark sea. They can dive deeper than any other mammal and stay underwater for twenty-five minutes! No narwhal has ever survived in captivity.

"That's odd," said Jack. "Most animals live longer in captivity. They get plenty of food, and they don't get killed by predators."

"I know," said Annie. "But when narwhals are captured and put in aquariums, they don't live long. They need to be free."

She and Jack watched the narwhals dive deeper into the water. Their large heart-shaped tails flashed above the surface. Then the creatures disappeared from sight. Jack read more:

Like most whales, narwhals communicate underwater by using a variety of sounds, such as clicks, whistles, and squeaks.

19

"Scientists put recorders in the sea," said Annie, "and they hear all these weird sounds. But they can't figure out what narwhals are saying, or how they can hear at such long distances."

"Look, they're back," said Jack.

The narwhals had popped to the surface. Several were swimming upside down. Some were pushing each other around. Others waved their tusks and tapped them together.

"Why are they tapping their tusks?" said Jack.

"They're having a chat," said Annie.

Jack laughed.

"Actually, scientists say they might use their tusks to attract mates or gather information," said Annie.

As Jack watched the narwhals bob up and down in the water, he tried to count them. "One, two, three, four . . ."

In the middle of his count, seabirds began to screech overhead. The narwhals made loud *whoosh-ing* sounds. They thrashed around in the water.

"What's wrong?" said Annie.

"That!" said Jack.

A tall fin was gliding across the bay. It looked like a black flag.

"A shark?" cried Annie.

"No, that's *way* bigger than a shark fin!" said Jack.

Suddenly a giant whale burst out of the waves. It had a black back and a white belly. It was as big as a school bus! The whale crashed down into the water.

"An orca—a killer whale!" cried Annie.

"And there's more than one!" said Jack.

At least four other giant black fins appeared in the bay. The killer whales were headed straight for the herd of narwhals.

4

STAND BACK!

"Go, guys, go!" Annie shouted to the narwhals. She raced to the shoreline.

Jack ran with her. "GO! GO! GO!" he yelled as loudly as he could.

The narwhals dove under the surface of the water again.

The orcas took off after them. But one of the huge predators swam toward Jack and Annie.

"Whoa!" said Jack, pulling Annie back from the edge of the sea.

Suddenly there was a flurry of splashes and *whoosh*ing sounds.

"What's happening?" said Jack.

"That orca's chasing a narwhal!" cried Annie.

A small narwhal had separated from his herd. He was swimming toward a row of icebergs about thirty feet offshore.

"The orca's still coming!" said Annie.

The giant orca kept chasing the narwhal.

"Hurry!" cried Jack.

The narwhal escaped through a passage in the row of icebergs. He swam into a pool of shallow water.

The orca was too big to swim through the opening. It crashed against the huge mounds of ice. Some of the ice splintered and broke off in chunks.

The orca tried to swim under the icebergs. But the water was too shallow. It smashed against the barrier again. But the passage was still too narrow.

Finally, the killer whale swam away.

"Yay!" said Annie. Jack sighed with relief.

The narwhal was alone in the pool of water.

"They're gone!" Jack called to him. "You can go now! Go!"

"Hurry! Before they come back!" yelled Annie.

"Find your friends!" shouted Jack.

As they spoke, more ice shifted and fell. A chunk of fallen ice now completely blocked the passage that led back out to deep water.

The narwhal circled inside the shallow pool. Surrounded by packed ice, he was trapped.

"Oh, no, he can't get out!" said Annie.

"Stand back!" someone shouted behind them. "Move away!"

Jack and Annie whirled around.

A boy with shoulder-length red hair stood on some rocks above them. He looked as young as Annie, but he was holding a huge spear.

"Whoa, hi!" said Jack. "Who are you?"

25

The boy scowled. He wore a red tunic with a rope around his waist, leather pants, and boots. His spear was made of wood and had a sharp metal blade.

Maybe his parents work at a research station, thought Jack. *Maybe he likes to dress in costumes and play with ancient weapons.*

"Move away! He is mine!" the boy said.

"What do you mean, *yours*?" said Jack.

"He's not anybody's!" said Annie.

The boy strode down the slope toward the water. He raised his spear, aiming it at the narwhal.

"No! Stop! What are you doing?" said Jack. He charged at the boy and tried to take his spear away. The boy lost his grip and dropped it.

Jack grabbed the spear. It was so heavy, he could barely lift it. *What kind of kid carries around something like this?* he wondered.

27

"Give it back!" the boy said. He reached for his spear. But Annie jumped between him and Jack.

"Stop!" she said. "Why do you want to hurt that narwhal? What's wrong with you?"

"His horn is worth a fortune. Everyone knows that," said the boy.

"That's a *terrible* reason!" said Annie.

"You can't kill him for his horn!" said Jack.

"Why not?" said the boy. He stared at Jack with fierce blue eyes.

"Because narwhals are special!" said Annie. "They're mysteries of nature. They know secrets we'll never know. They hear things in ways we'll never hear! They talk in a language we'll never understand! Get it?"

The boy looked from Jack to Annie. He took a deep breath and stepped to the water's edge. He stared at the narwhal as if seeing the creature for the first time.

Then he turned back to Jack and Annie.

"I will help you free him," he said.

"Thank you!" said Annie.

"Here, you can have this back," said Jack. He gave the boy his spear.

"How can we free him?" asked Annie.

"We will go to him together," said the boy. "Come with me."

5

Erik's Son

Jack and Annie followed the boy up the rocky slope and down the other side.

There was a wooden rowboat on the shore. It looked like it had been made by hand. Two oars were inside.

The boy put his spear into the boat, then pushed it halfway into the water. "Sit at this end," he said.

"Thanks," said Annie. She and Jack climbed into the rowboat. They sat together on a wooden seat.

The boy pushed the boat farther into the water.

Then he jumped aboard and sat in the center, facing Jack and Annie.

He grasped the oars. He looked over his shoulder to see where to go. Then he pulled the oars through the water, and the rowboat began moving away from shore.

The wind had picked up, and the water was choppy. The rowboat rocked from side to side.

"Hold on tightly," the boy said. "If we fall in, we freeze to death."

Jack gripped the side of the boat as it bumped through the waves.

The boy rowed around a bend in the bay. Then he headed toward the ice barrier trapping the narwhal. He rowed close to a wide, flat chunk of ice.

"Hey, you!" Annie called to the whale. "Don't be afraid!"

The narwhal was still swimming in circles. He had a cone-shaped body and short front flippers. His long ivory tusk looked like twisted rope.

"We've come to help you!" said Annie.

"We need to break up that piece of the ice," the boy said to Jack. He pointed to the chunk that was blocking the narwhal's escape.

"Right," said Jack. "How do we do that?"

"Sit here. Hold the boat steady," said the boy. He made room for Jack to sit next to him on the center seat. Then he handed Jack the oars.

Jack grasped the wooden handles and tried to keep the boat from tipping over.

The boy carefully stood up. He stepped out

onto the flat ice surface. The boat rocked, but Jack used the oars to keep it close to the ice.

The boy started kicking the ice chunks. He kicked and kicked.

Suddenly he slipped and fell hard onto the icy surface. He clutched his right knee and groaned.

"Are you okay?" said Annie.

"Yes," said the boy. He tried to stand up, but he groaned again and sat back on the ice.

"Wait! I can help!" said Annie.

Jack held the boat steady as Annie climbed out. She kicked the fallen ice chunk, but it didn't move.

"Use the spear!" said Jack. He let go of the oars long enough to pick up the boy's spear.

"Use it how?" said Annie.

"Just take it." Jack held the spear out to her. "Careful, it's super heavy."

Annie took the spear with both hands.

"Slide it between the chunk of ice and the big iceberg," said Jack.

Annie wedged the spear between the two solid
blocks of ice.

"Got it?" said Jack. "Now pull back."

Annie pulled hard on the spear.

"I can help," said the boy. Even though he was

injured, he stood up. He gripped the spear with Annie, and they pulled together.

Bit by bit, the ice began to splinter against the steel blade of the spear.

Annie and the boy kept pushing and pulling—

until the fallen chunk of ice finally popped free, like a cork popping out of a bottle.

The narwhal kept circling the shallow pool.

"This way!" Annie called to him. She pointed to the gap in the ice. "Swim through there!"

The narwhal seemed to understand. He looked at Annie, then turned and shot out through the passage.

Jack and Annie raised their arms above their heads and shook their fists. "Yay!" they shouted.

The boy looked at them. Then he raised his arms, too, and shook his fists. "Yay!" he said.

Jack and Annie laughed, and the boy laughed with them. For the first time, he seemed like a regular kid, Jack thought.

The three of them watched the narwhal swim away and disappear into deep water.

The boy smiled at Jack and Annie. "You both are strong and smart," he said.

"Thanks," they said together.

"Are you sure you're okay?" said Jack.

"Yes," said the boy.

"What's your name?" said Annie.

"Erikson," said the boy. "My father is Erik."

"Oh, I get it—your dad is Erik, so you are called *Erik-son*!" said Annie.

"Yes," said Erikson.

"My name is Jack," said Jack. "And she's my sister, Annie."

"Where do you live?" asked Erikson.

"Far away. We're just visiting Greenland for the day," said Annie. "Do you live around here?"

"Yes," said the boy. "Would you like to meet my family?"

"Sure!" said Annie.

"Absolutely," said Jack.

Annie climbed back into the rowboat. The boy limped to the edge of the ice.

"Do you need help rowing?" asked Jack.

"No, thank you. I can still do it," the boy said.

Jack carefully stood up. He gave Erikson his hand and helped him into the boat. Then Jack took his seat next to Annie.

Erikson picked up the oars. He looked over his shoulder and began rowing through the ice-cold seawater.

6

THE MIST OF TIME

As Erikson rowed across the bay, the waves were rough. But his oar strokes were strong and steady.

"So where do you live?" Jack asked, rocking from side to side.

"Erik's Inlet." The boy nodded to a place between the steep hills where the sea flowed in.

"Did people name it for your father?" said Annie.

"No," said Erikson. "My father named it for himself."

"Does he work at one of the research stations?" Jack asked.

Erikson looked puzzled.

"I mean, is he a scientist?" asked Jack.

The boy shook his head. "He is a sailor," he said.

"Oh. Cool," said Jack.

"I am a seafarer, too," said Erikson. "Soon I will sail away on my own."

Annie laughed, as if she thought he was kidding.

Jack didn't know what to think. He liked Erikson, but he couldn't figure him out. The boy's manner, his spear, and his outfit were really odd. *And who says* seafarer *anymore?* Jack wondered.

Erikson rowed through the choppy waters and into Erik's Inlet. The hills on either side of the narrow water passage sparkled with ice and snow.

As the boat moved along the inlet, clouds covered the sky. The air grew foggy. Soon it was hard to see where they were. Jack could hear seabirds cawing, but he couldn't see them. Icebergs drifted close to the rowboat. They looked like ghost ships.

"Spooky," said Jack.

"Yeah," Annie whispered. "But we're doing what our rhyme says to do."

On a day that seems endless,
With no dark of night,
Travel through fog.
Travel through light.

"Right, we are," said Jack. "But I still don't know what *no dark of night* means."

Before Annie could answer, a bellowing noise came from up ahead.

"What's that?" said Jack.

The rowboat moved past a flat iceberg. Through the fog, a huge animal loomed into view. The creature was as big as a polar bear. It had two long tusks.

41

"A walrus!" said Jack.

The walrus had bushy whiskers, a broad head, and flippers. Its wrinkled skin was the color of cinnamon.

"Hi, mister!" said Annie with a laugh. "I didn't know walruses were so big!"

Erikson rowed on. He steered the boat between sheets of floating ice. Two ringed seals rested on one sheet. Seagulls were perched on another.

"Look, a reindeer!" said Annie.

Through the fog, Jack saw a delicate-looking deer on the shore. Its antlers looked like tall tree branches.

"You're beautiful!" called Annie.

The reindeer dipped its head shyly.

"She said thanks," said Annie. "Did you know reindeer are also called *caribou*?"

"Cool," said Jack.

"And their noses warm the cold air before it goes to their lungs," said Annie.

"Like Rudolph the Red-Nosed Reindeer," said Jack with a laugh. "Did you write a report on reindeer, too?"

"No," said Annie. "I just really love learning stuff like that."

Jack smiled. Annie knew more about animals

43

than anyone. She could talk to them and hear them in special ways.

As Erikson rowed down the river of seawater, the fog cleared. The clouds drifted off. The cliffs and the waves sparkled with sunlight again.

Soon they passed low hills and greenish-brown fields. There was less ice and snow. A few trees dotted the land. Sheep were scattered across the hillsides.

"Oh, this is so beautiful!" Annie said. "Has your family lived in Greenland for a long time?"

"Eight years," said Erikson. "We began the voyage from Iceland with twenty-five ships. But eleven ships did not make it."

"Are you serious?" said Jack.

"Yes," said Erikson.

"That's so sad!" said Annie.

Jack was confused. What year was this?

"Everyone knew the journey would be hard,"

said the boy. He looked over his shoulder as he rowed around a curve.

"This is where we live," he said as the boat glided into a sheltered cove.

"Wow," breathed Annie.

Anchored along the water's edge were fourteen ships. They were long, slender sailing ships made of wood. Dragon heads were carved into their prows.

Jack gasped. He'd seen ships just like these before—they were *Viking* ships.

Suddenly Jack understood what had happened. He and Annie had come to Greenland in the time of Vikings—*about a thousand years ago!*

7

ANOTHER WORLD

Lots of things made sense to Jack now—Erikson's clothes, his spear, calling himself a seafarer, and his story of eleven ships lost while sailing from Iceland to Greenland.

Erikson rowed toward a small wooden pier near the Viking ships. When the boat reached the shore, he jumped out.

"We are here!" he said.

Jack and Annie climbed carefully out of the boat. As Erikson tied it to the pier, Jack turned to Annie.

"Those are Viking ships!" he whispered. "We

saw ships like that on our mission to Ireland. Remember? Viking raiders were invading the coast!"

"Yikes!" said Annie, her eyes wide.

"We should escape now while we can," said Jack.

"Wait, wait, let's look at the rhyme," said Annie.

Jack slipped the rhyme out of his bag.

Annie pointed to the last verse. They read silently:

Explore different worlds.
Show friends where to go.
Unite all these worlds
With a word that will glow.

"I think we're doing what Morgan wants," Annie said. "We explored the world of seals and orcas and narwhals . . . and now *this* world, the Viking world."

47

"But what about—" Jack started.

"Shh!" said Annie.

Erikson had finished tying up the boat. Jack put the rhyme back into his bag.

"Follow me," Erikson said.

Even though he was still limping, Erikson walked faster than Jack and Annie. He bounded across the rocky shore and started up a hill.

Jack and Annie hurried after him. Soon they could see a cluster of buildings over the crest of the hill.

There was a long wooden house and smaller thatched huts and several barns. A few people were working in the chilly sunlight. They were all dressed in several layers of clothing.

Women were hanging clothes to dry. Men were stacking wood.

A boy was leading cows to a barn. A few girls were feeding hogs and ducks. Chickens and dogs wandered about.

Suddenly the dogs began to bark. Everyone looked around. A woman cried out and pointed at Jack and Annie.

Two brown-and-white dogs bolted down the hill, barking ferociously.

Erikson shouted a command. The dogs stopped barking.

A tall, burly man strode down the slope.

"My father," said Erikson.

Erikson's father had long red hair and a wild, bushy beard. He carried an ax.

"Oh, no," whispered Jack. The Viking man looked fierce.

"Wait here," Erikson ordered Jack and Annie. Leaving them with the dogs, he limped to his father. Jack nervously watched him speak to the wild-looking man.

"How are you guys doing today?" Annie asked the dogs.

The dogs barked.

"Oh, you're just pretending to be scary," she said.

The dogs tilted their heads, then started to pant. Their tails were wagging.

Annie laughed and held out her hand for the dogs to sniff. Their sniffing quickly turned into licking.

Erikson and his father walked down to Jack and Annie.

"This is my father. Erik," the boy said. "He is the chieftain here."

"Oh. Uh . . . hello . . . sir," said Jack.

"Glad to meet you!" said Annie.

"Where do you come from?" Erikson's father asked in a deep voice.

"Frog Creek, Pennsylvania," said Jack.

"In the United States of America," Annie added.

"You might not have heard of it," Jack said quickly.

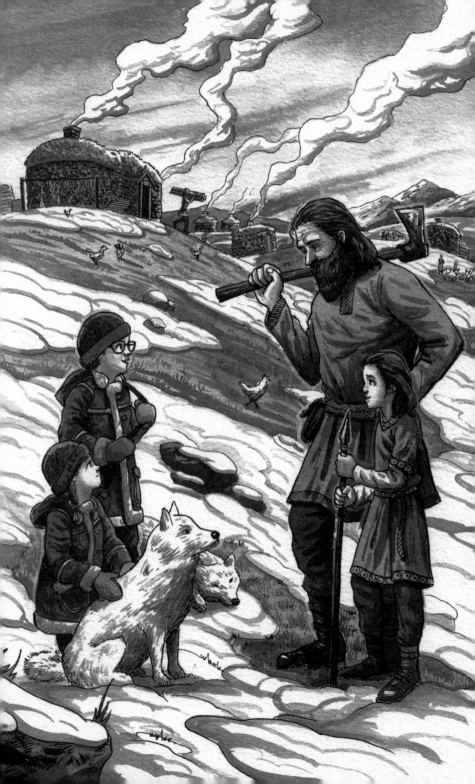

"No, I have not. Where is that?" Erik asked gruffly.

"It's on the continent of North America," said Annie.

Oh, no, thought Jack. He knew the Vikings hadn't yet heard of the United States or North America. In Erik's time, the United States wouldn't be a country for another 700 years!

But Erik just nodded. "So you are from far away?" he said.

"Yes," said Annie.

"Welcome," said Erik. He turned to his son. "Leif, let us take your friends to the house."

"Thanks!" said Annie. Then she and Jack started up the hill, following the boy and his father.

Erik called the boy Leif, Jack thought. *Leif? . . . Leif Erikson? . . . LEIF ERIKSON!*

"Annie," he whispered. "Erikson's *first name* is *Leif*!"

"I heard that," she said. "Erikson must be his last name."

"Yes! I've read about Leif Erikson and Erik the Red," said Jack. "They're famous!"

"Famous?" said Annie.

"Uh, yeah!" said Jack. "They're two of the most famous explorers in the history of the world!"

8

*A*ROUND THE *F*IRE

"*A*re you serious?" said Annie.

"Leif was the first European to step onto the North American continent," said Jack, "five hundred years before Christopher Columbus."

"No way," breathed Annie.

"Yes way!" said Jack.

"Come along!" Erik called from farther up the hill.

Annie and Jack hurried to catch up with Leif and his father.

"So . . . you're Erik the Red and Leif Erikson?" Annie asked excitedly.

"Yes," Erik said.

Before Annie could say more, Jack changed the subject. "Why did you decide to live here in Greenland?" he said.

"I wanted a new life," Erik said. "People call us pirates. But I am a seafarer who searches for safe harbors where I can live with my family. I have found one here at the edge of the world. I named it Greenland."

"Why?" asked Annie. "I mean, why'd you call it that?"

"Because the word is nice, is it not?" said Erik with a wink. "I hoped it would make others want to come live here, too."

The small group of people watched as Jack and Annie climbed to the top of the hill with Leif and Erik.

One of the women in the group stepped forward. She had long blond braids and a kind face.

"Who are these children, my son?" she said to Leif.

"My new friends, Jack and Annie," said Leif. "They come from far away."

Leif's mother smiled. "Welcome, Jack and Annie. Come share our dinner with us," she said. She led them to the largest house on the hill. It was a long stone house with a steep roof made of grass.

Leif's mother ushered Jack and Annie through the door. She took Jack's and Annie's hats, gloves, and coats. She put them on a bench near the door. Jack put his wool bag there, too.

The Viking house was dark and warm inside. Lit only with oil lamps, the windowless house was one long narrow room. In the center was a fire pit. Smoke rose through a hole in the roof. The house smelled of fish and grease and animal fur.

Erik and Leif sat on low stools near the fire.

"Sit, warm yourselves," Erik said. Jack and Annie sat down with them.

Leif's mother stirred a black pot over the fire. Then she ladled food into stone bowls and gave them to everyone, along with wooden spoons.

"Thank you," said Jack and Annie.

The food in the bowl looked like a milky gray mush. Jack was afraid to taste it. But when he did, he actually liked it. It tasted like oatmeal.

"Did you sail here with your family and friends?" Erik asked them as they ate.

"No, it's just us," said Annie. "Jack and me."

"But how is that possible?" said Erik. "How did two children find their way here alone?"

"Uh . . . well . . ." Jack didn't know what to say.

"We have a map," said Annie.

"A map?" said Erik.

"A map!" said Leif. "May we see it?"

"Sure," said Jack. He put down his bowl and grabbed his bag. He took out their map. He unfolded it and held it up for them to see.

Leif and his parents stared in silent wonder.

"Our land is south of here," said Jack, pointing. "It's a long way south. It's . . . well . . . it's off the map."

"So you used this map to come to Greenland in your ship?" asked Erik.

"Uh . . . we came in the tree house," said Annie.

"'Tree House'? That is the name of your ship?" asked Erik.

"Well . . . sort of," said Jack. "It's not much of a ship. But you guys have really *great* ships. We saw—"

"Wait. *Your* ship must be the best in the world," said Erik. "Two children sailed it alone to

60

Greenland! I would like very much to see a ship such as yours."

"Oh." Jack caught his breath.

"Let us go see it now!" Erik stood up.

"Um . . . can we please wait until morning?" Annie said. "We're pretty tired."

"Erik, let the children rest," Leif's mother said. "In the morning, we will all go—the whole village will go—to see their wondrous ship. Come, Jack and Annie." She picked up an oil lamp.

They all stood.

"Good night," Annie said to Leif and Erik.

Jack put their map back into his bag. Then he and Annie followed Leif's mother to a shadowy end of the house.

"You may sleep here," she said. She pointed to two fur-covered benches against the wall.

"Thank you," said Annie. She and Jack climbed onto the benches, and Leif's mother covered them with more soft furs.

"Rest well," she said. "Keep the lamp burning so you will not be afraid." She put the oil lamp on a small table. Then she left them.

"Jack," whispered Annie. "We don't have a ship to show them."

"I know," he said. "We'd better leave soon. After everyone goes to bed, we can sneak away. . . ."

"Right," said Annie. "We can borrow Leif's rowboat." She yawned.

"It'll be dark outside . . . ," said Jack, trying to keep his eyes open. "How will we find our way?"

"We can worry about that later," said Annie.

"Right . . . ," said Jack, closing his eyes. "Let's just rest until Leif and his parents go to bed. . . . Stay awake. . . . Don't go to . . ."

Before Jack could say *sleep*, he dropped off to sleep.

9

THE MIDNIGHT SUN

"Jack," Annie whispered. "Wake up!"

Jack rubbed his eyes. "Where is everyone?" he asked.

"I just checked. They're asleep at the other end of the house," said Annie. "We have to go."

"Now?" said Jack. "Maybe we should wait till daylight...."

"No, they might get up before then," said Annie.

"You're right," said Jack. He threw off the warm fur and sat up.

"Let's go," said Annie. She picked up the burning oil lamp. Jack grabbed his bag.

As they crept to the door, snoring came from the other end of the long house.

They stopped at the bench by the door. In the dim light of the lamp, they put on their coats and hats and mittens.

"We should write a note to Leif," whispered Jack.

"Good idea," said Annie.

Jack pulled out his notebook and pencil from his bag. "How's this?" He whispered as he wrote:

> Dear Leif, we had to leave suddenly. We are borrowing your rowboat to go back to the bay. We will leave it where we met you. Many thanks to you and your family.

"Perfect," said Annie. "And let's leave him our map since he liked it so much."

"Good idea," breathed Jack. He tore the note from the notebook and placed it on the bench with their map.

Jack and Annie pulled on their gloves. Then Annie opened the door, and they slipped out of the house.

It was freezing outside. But to Jack's surprise, it was sunny!

"What time is it?" he said. "I thought it was night."

"Me too," said Annie. "But no one's around—not even the dogs. Hurry!"

Jack and Annie took off down the hill. In the cold, windy sunlight, they hurried to the shore.

Small waves were splashing against the moored Viking ships. Leif's rowboat was tied to the pier near them.

Jack and Annie stepped onto the pier, and Jack untied the rope. Just as he and Annie were about to climb aboard, someone yelled, "Stop!"

"Oh, no!" said Annie.

Leif was limping down the hill toward them. He held their note and map in his hand.

"I heard you leave!" he called. "Then I read your message. I must take you to your ship. It is not easy to row in windy waters."

"But your knee still hurts. I can tell," said Annie.

Leif shrugged. "That is not important," he said. "We should go quickly so I can return before morning."

"Morning? I thought it was morning now," said Jack.

"It is close to midnight," Leif said. "You have come in the time of the midnight sun."

"I get it," Annie said to Jack. *On a day that seems endless, with no dark of night.*

"Right," said Jack. Now he remembered the Midnight Sun! In the far north, the summer sun can still be seen at midnight.

"Here, you forgot this," said Leif. He thrust the map and note into Jack's hands. "You will need your map to sail your ship home."

"No, we won't," said Jack. "We know the way. You need it more." He handed the map back to Leif.

"Oh!" Leif stared at the map as if it were made of gold. "I cannot believe you would give this to me," he said in a hushed voice. "Thank you very much."

"No problem," said Annie.

Leif smiled. "Let us go!" he said.

Jack put the note into his coat pocket. Then he and Annie climbed aboard.

Leif sat across from them. He began rowing through the choppy water.

"Tell me about your land," he said. "What is it like?"

"It has everything," said Annie. "Mountains and valleys and oceans and rivers."

"And lakes and forests and grassy plains," said Jack, "and farms, small towns, and *huge* towns called cities."

With the wind at their backs, Leif rowed swiftly. The water was bathed in a gold mist.

Soon Leif rowed the boat from Erik's Inlet into the bay.

"You can drop us off there," said Jack. He pointed to the shore where they had saved the narwhal.

"But where is your ship?" asked Leif.

"Uh . . . I'm really sorry, but we promised the person who owns it that we would not show it to anyone," Annie said.

"I understand," said Leif, nodding. "We must always honor our promises."

"You should hurry home before your mom and

dad wake up," said Annie. "They'll be worried if they find you missing."

"Yes," said Leif, smiling. "They will think I have sailed away with you. They know I am eager to travel to faraway places."

Leif rowed to the shore, and Jack and Annie hopped out of the boat.

"Good-bye," the Viking boy said. "I thank you again for your map. I promise I will make good use of it."

"And *I* promise you will have great success!" said Jack.

"Do you think so?" said Leif.

"Absolutely!" said Annie.

Leif raised his arms above his head and clenched his fists. "Yay!" he said.

Jack and Annie laughed.

Leif waved good-bye. Using his oars, he pushed his boat offshore.

"I hope your knee feels better soon!" called Annie.

"I have already forgotten about it!" Leif called back. Then he rowed away through the soft light of the Arctic night.

"Leif's really tough and brave," said Annie. "He'll make a good explorer."

"Yeah, a great one," said Jack. He took a deep breath. "I guess we can go now."

Jack and Annie walked around the bend in the shore.

Annie gasped. "Jack! Look!" she said.

"What?" said Jack.

"There—in the water—at the edge of the ice," said Annie.

"A narwhal!" whispered Jack.

"Yes!" said Annie. "*Our* narwhal!"

10

A Word That Glows

"Hi! You're back!" said Annie.

The narwhal was about ten feet away. He was swimming near a sheet of ice that jutted out from the shore. His ivory tusk was pointed at them.

"Is something wrong with him?" said Jack. "Why is he here?"

"He wants to tell us something," said Annie.

"How do you know?" said Jack.

"I just know," said Annie. "I'm going out to him. I'll crawl on the ice."

"No, don't!" said Jack. "It could crack."

"Don't worry, it's really thick," said Annie. "It's probably been here for thousands of years."

Annie stepped out onto the packed ice. Then she got on her hands and knees and began crawling toward the narwhal.

"Careful!" said Jack.

"I got it," said Annie, reaching the edge of the ice.

The narwhal raised his head above the water.

"Hi, you! What's up?" said Annie, grinning. "Why did you come back?"

The narwhal made noises that sounded like a door creaking. Then he tapped Annie's head with his unicorn horn.

Annie laughed. "Thank *you*!" she said.

The narwhal then turned and swam away. He soon disappeared under the water.

Annie crawled back toward Jack. She stepped off the ice sheet onto the shore.

"That was so cool," she said.

"What happened?" said Jack.

"Simple," said Annie. "He came back to thank us."

"You're kidding," said Jack.

"Nope," said Annie. "That's basically what he said: *Thanks.* And then I said *thanks* back."

"That's all?" said Jack.

"That's enough," said Annie.

Jack took a deep breath. "Okay! *Now* we can leave!"

He and Annie quickly walked over the slope. The tree house was still sitting on the pebbly shore. It was lit by the orange and red light of the Midnight Sun. Jack and Annie slipped through the window.

Annie grabbed the Pennsylvania book that

always took them home. She pointed to a photo of the Frog Creek woods. "I wish we could go there!"

Nothing happened. The wind did not start to blow.

"I wish we could go there!" Annie said again.

The wind still did not start to blow.

"Why aren't we leaving?" said Jack.

"Let's look at our rhyme," said Annie, "at the last verse."

Jack pulled the rhyme out of his bag. He read aloud:

Explore different worlds.
Show friends where to go.

"Okay! We did that!" said Annie. "We showed our friends where to go—we gave Leif our map! And we showed the narwhal how to escape from the shallow water!"

"Yeah, we *did* all that," said Jack. "And I wasn't even thinking about the rhyme!"

"Read the rest," said Annie.

Jack read the last two lines:

Unite all these worlds
With a word that will glow.

"I forgot about those lines, too," said Jack. "What do they mean? What's the word?"

"I don't know. But if it glows, it must be written down somewhere," said Annie. "Check your notebook."

Jack pulled out his notebook, and he and Annie looked at it together.

"Oh, man. I forgot to take any notes," said Jack. "What about our Greenland book?" He took out the Greenland book and thumbed through it. "Nothing glowing here."

"Wait, what about our message to Leif's family?" said Annie.

Jack reached into his pocket and pulled out the crumpled note. He and Annie looked at it together.

"Nothing," said Jack.

"Hold on!" said Annie. "Look at the letter **T**!"

Annie pointed at the letter **T** near the bottom of their note. The letter seemed a little brighter than the other letters. Then suddenly it glowed like it was on fire. Next to the **T**, the letter **H** grew brighter. Then **A** grew brighter. Then the next letter, **N**.

One by one, the letters grew brighter—until **T-H-A-N-K-S** was all aglow.

"Thanks!" cried Annie. "That's the word!"

"Thanks?" said Jack. "Why *thanks*?"

"I'll explain when we get back," said Annie. "We can go now."

Annie pointed at the picture of Frog Creek again. "I wish we could go there!"

The wind started to blow.

"Yay! It worked!" said Jack.

The tree house started to spin.

It spun faster and faster.

Then everything was still.

Absolutely still.

11

You!

Warm air filled the tree house. No time at all had passed in Frog Creek. The sky was dark blue. The first stars were out. Jack and Annie were wearing their summer clothes again.

"Welcome home," said Annie.

Jack sighed with relief. Frog Creek seemed especially nice in the soft twilight. The woods smelled of green trees and green plants.

"Let's go," said Jack. He left Morgan's rhyme, the Greenland book, and their note for Leif on the floor of the tree house.

Then he put his notebook into his backpack and headed down the rope ladder. Annie followed.

As Jack and Annie started through the woods, the air was filled with the sounds of crickets and tree frogs.

"So, do you get it about *thanks*?" Annie asked.

"Uh . . . sort of, but it seems so ordinary," said Jack. "People say it all the time and they don't even think about it."

"Exactly!" said Annie. "So, let's think about it."

"Okay . . . ," said Jack.

"You say thanks when someone helps you or is nice to you or gives you a gift, right?" said Annie.

"Yeah," said Jack.

"Leif helped us free the narwhal. And we said thanks," said Annie. "His parents gave us food, and we said thanks. We gave Leif our map, and he said thanks. The narwhal came back and said thanks. And I thanked him for thanking us and for just being amazing."

"Got it," said Jack. "But what does *thanks* do?"

Annie took a deep breath. "Okay. This is the important part," she said. "When the Vikings say thanks to us and we thank them, our world joins with their world. We *unite* our worlds, like the rhyme said. Two worlds, a thousand years apart, come together."

"Whoa. That's cool," said Jack.

Jack and Annie came out of the woods and started down the sidewalk.

"There's more," said Annie. Her eyes were shining. "When the narwhal says thanks, our world joins with *his* world, a world in the darkest deep sea no one knows much about. But if people really knew how to thank narwhals just for being amazing and how to hear *their* thanks, it could change everything . . . like, it might save them if they're ever in danger. . . ." She sounded close to tears. "Do you get it now?"

"Yeah . . . I do actually," said Jack. "Thanks to you."

"No, thanks to *you*," said Annie.

"No, *you*," said Jack.

"You!" said Annie.

"You, you, you!" said Jack.

"Thanks to BOTH OF US!" shouted Annie.

"Come on, we're late," said Jack.

He and Annie ran down their dark street. They crossed their yard. They dashed up the porch steps and banged through the front door.

"Mom! Dad! We're home!" shouted Annie.

"Thanks for everything!" yelled Jack.

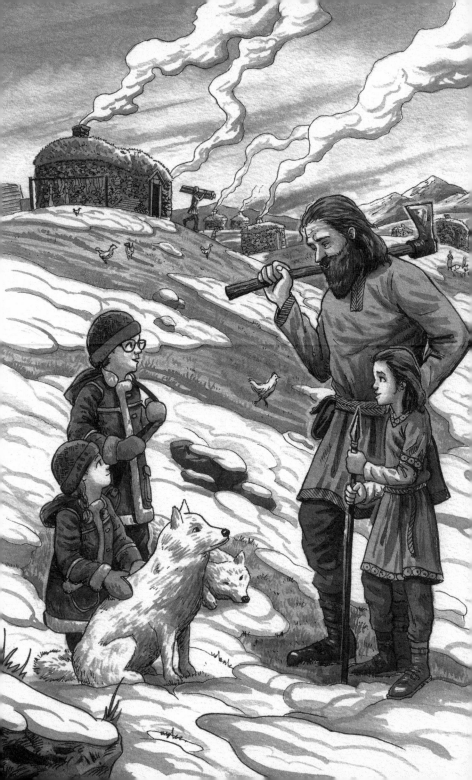

AUTHOR'S NOTE

Fact:

Erik the Red was a famous Viking explorer. Around AD 982, he was the first European to discover Greenland.

Erik's son Leif Erikson (known as Leif the Lucky) led the first European expedition to the mainland of North America, 500 years before Christopher Columbus.

Fiction:

Jack and Annie gave Leif a map to help him get there.

Turn the page for a sneak peek at

Magic Tree House® Fact Tracker

Narwhals and Other Whales

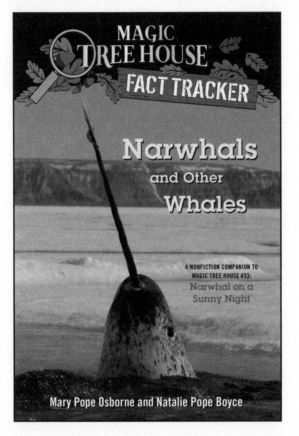

Studying the Arctic Ocean takes a lot of planning. Some scientists work in stations built right on the ice. They must

Waterproof backpack

Tent

Insulated rubber boots

Hiking boots

Hand and foot warmers

Sunglasses with straps

Padded rain jacket

Three-layer rain pants

Heavy socks

Fleece jackets

have snowmobiles, ice drills, and lots of
research equipment, as well as food and
medicine to last for months.

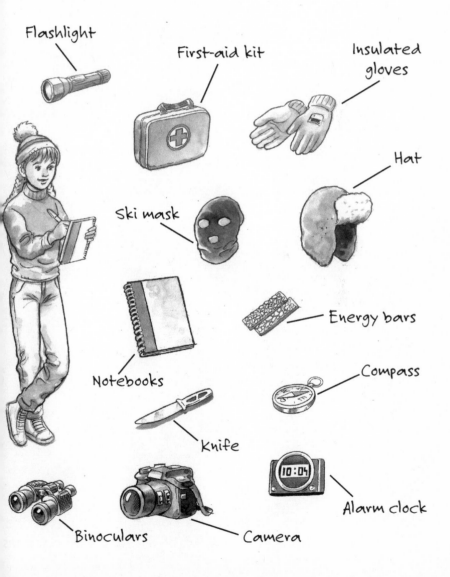

Flashlight

First-aid kit

Insulated gloves

Hat

Ski mask

Energy bars

Notebooks

Compass

Knife

Alarm clock

Binoculars

Camera

Young, Older, Oldest!

By studying the lens of a narwhal's eye, researchers can usually tell its age. Based on this, they think that narwhals can live to be ninety or even one hundred years old!

The color of a narwhal's skin is another

Baby whales are called <u>calves</u>.

way to guess its age. Young narwhals are pale blue and gray. As they get older, their skin becomes darker and has dark spots on it. As time passes, the spots grow whiter. Old narwhals are totally white. To some people they seem like sea ghosts quietly gliding by.

Belugas Adopt a Narwhal

In 2016, a young narwhal was spotted swimming with a pod of young beluga males in the St. Lawrence River in Canada. No one knows why, but he had strayed about six hundred miles south of his Arctic home.

Belugas and narwhals are close relatives, and the belugas seemed to have adopted the narwhal into their pod. All the whales were bumping against one another and playing together. The narwhal even started blowing bubbles like his beluga pals! As of 2018, the narwhal was still swimming with the belugas.

Yang Yun and Mila

Yang Yun was a young Chinese woman learning to work with whales at an aquarium in Harbin, China. In 2009, she and some other students tried to see how long they could hold their breath underwater.

There were some beluga whales in the tank with them. The water was twenty feet deep and icy cold. Yun began to have terrible leg cramps. She found it impossible to move her legs and started to sink to the bottom. She knew she was in serious trouble when she couldn't get any air and began to swallow water and choke.

Suddenly there was a strong force pushing her up to the surface. It was Mila, one of the belugas! She had Yun's leg in her mouth! People watching were stunned as Mila pushed Yun up to safety. She was saved by a whale!

Humpback Whale

Humpback whales are huge gray animals that weigh up to 80,000 pounds and are forty to fifty feet long. They get their name because they hump their backs up when they dive.

Humpbacks spend summers at the North and South Poles. Then they head to warmer waters in places like Mexico and Hawaii. They don't eat all winter and survive on the fat stored in their bodies.

Humpbacks swim the longest distance of all whales. They cover about 16,000 miles going back and forth between their summer and winter homes. They sing as they swim. Their songs might be heard many miles away!

Humpbacks can go four months without food.

Blue Whale

Blue whales live at the North and South Poles in the summer and in warmer waters in the winter. They are the largest creatures ever to have lived on earth and can be up to 100 feet long and weigh about 300,000 pounds!

Their heart alone weighs about 1,000 pounds . . . that's the size of a small car!

And their tongue is as heavy as an elephant! Isn't it amazing that these animals feed on sea creatures the size of your fingernail?

Blue whales are one of the loudest animals on the planet. When one makes noise, the sound travels miles through the water. It's louder than a jet engine!

Magic Tree House®

Magic Tree House® Merlin Missions

Magic Tree House® Super Edition

#1: WORLD AT WAR, 1944

Magic Tree House® Fact Trackers

DINOSAURS

KNIGHTS AND CASTLES

MUMMIES AND PYRAMIDS

PIRATES

RAIN FORESTS

SPACE

TITANIC

TWISTERS AND OTHER TERRIBLE STORMS

DOLPHINS AND SHARKS

ANCIENT GREECE AND THE OLYMPICS

AMERICAN REVOLUTION

SABERTOOTHS AND THE ICE AGE

PILGRIMS

ANCIENT ROME AND POMPEII

TSUNAMIS AND OTHER NATURAL DISASTERS

POLAR BEARS AND THE ARCTIC

SEA MONSTERS

PENGUINS AND ANTARCTICA

LEONARDO DA VINCI

GHOSTS

LEPRECHAUNS AND IRISH FOLKLORE

RAGS AND RICHES: KIDS IN THE TIME OF
  CHARLES DICKENS

SNAKES AND OTHER REPTILES

DOG HEROES

ABRAHAM LINCOLN

PANDAS AND OTHER ENDANGERED SPECIES

HORSE HEROES

HEROES FOR ALL TIMES

SOCCER

NINJAS AND SAMURAI

CHINA: LAND OF THE EMPEROR'S GREAT
  WALL

SHARKS AND OTHER PREDATORS

VIKINGS

DOGSLEDDING AND EXTREME SPORTS

DRAGONS AND MYTHICAL CREATURES

WORLD WAR II

BASEBALL

WILD WEST

TEXAS

WARRIORS

BENJAMIN FRANKLIN

NARWHALS AND OTHER WHALES

More Magic Tree House®

GAMES AND PUZZLES FROM THE TREE HOUSE

MAGIC TRICKS FROM THE TREE HOUSE

MY MAGIC TREE HOUSE JOURNAL

MAGIC TREE HOUSE SURVIVAL GUIDE

ANIMAL GAMES AND PUZZLES

MAGIC TREE HOUSE INCREDIBLE FACT BOOK